ANIMAL BABIES

BABY DOGS

by Margaret Shanley

Consultant: Beth Gambro
Reading Specialist, Yorkville, Illinois

BEARPORT
PUBLISHING

Minneapolis, Minnesota

Teaching Tips

Before Reading

- Briefly discuss animal life cycles. Babies are born, they grow, and they have their own babies.
- Look through the glossary together. Read and discuss the words.
- Go on a picture walk, looking through the pictures to discuss vocabulary and make predictions about the text.

During Reading

- Encourage readers to point to each word as it is read. Stop occasionally to ask readers to point to a specific word in the text.
- If a reader encounters an unknown word, ask them to look at the rest of the page. Are there any clues to help them understand?

After Reading

- Check for understanding.
  - ▸ What are some things baby dogs do during the first few weeks? What about after that?
  - ▸ When does a puppy start eating solid food?
  - ▸ Look at page 22. What did you learn about baby dogs from reading this book?
- Ask the readers to think deeper.
  - ▸ Other than size, what is one thing that is different about baby dogs and adult dogs?
  - ▸ What is one thing that is similar about baby and adult dogs?

Credits:
Cover, © Anna Hoychuk/Shutterstock; 3, © Eric Isselee/Shutterstock; 4-5, © annamarias/Alamy; 6, © Alan Dyck/Dreamstime; 6-7, © art nick/Shutterstock; 8, © Anna Hoychuk/Shutterstock; 9, © ShannonDickerson/Shutterstock; 10-11, © Farinoza/Dreamstime; 12-13 , © Daniel Budiman/Dreamstime; 14-15, © © Anna Hoychuk/Shutterstock; 16, © Reddogs/Shutterstock; 16-17, © Susan Schmitz/Shutterstock; 18-19, © Erik Lam/Shutterstock; 20-21, © SolStock/iStock; 22, © squiremi/iStock; 23TL, © Christa Eder/Dreamstime; 23TM, © jzcz/Shutterstock; 23TR, © Ian Tragen/Shutterstock; 23BL, © anurakpong/iStock; 23BM, © William Wise/Dreamstime; and 23BR, © cynoclub/Shutterstock.

Library of Congress Cataloging-in-Publication Data

Names: Shanley, Margaret, 1972– author.
Title: Baby dogs / by Margaret Shanley.
Description: Bearcub books edition. | Minneapolis, Minnesota: Bearport
  Publishing Company, [2021] | Series: Animal babies | Includes
  bibliographical references and index.
Identifiers: LCCN 2020015858 (print) | LCCN 2020015859 (ebook) | ISBN
  9781642809558 (library binding) | ISBN 9781642809626 (paperback) | ISBN
  9781642809695 (ebook)
Subjects: LCSH: Puppies—Juvenile literature.
Classification: LCC SF426.5 .S517 2021 (print) | LCC SF426.5 (ebook) |
  DDC 636.7/07—dc23
LC record available at https://lccn.loc.gov/2020015858
LC ebook record available at https://lccn.loc.gov/2020015859

For more information, write to Bearport Publishing, 5357 Penn Avenue South, Minneapolis, MN 55419.

Printed in the United States of America.

Contents

It's a Baby Dog!

Lick!

The mother dog licks her **newborn** baby.

The puppy starts to **breathe**.

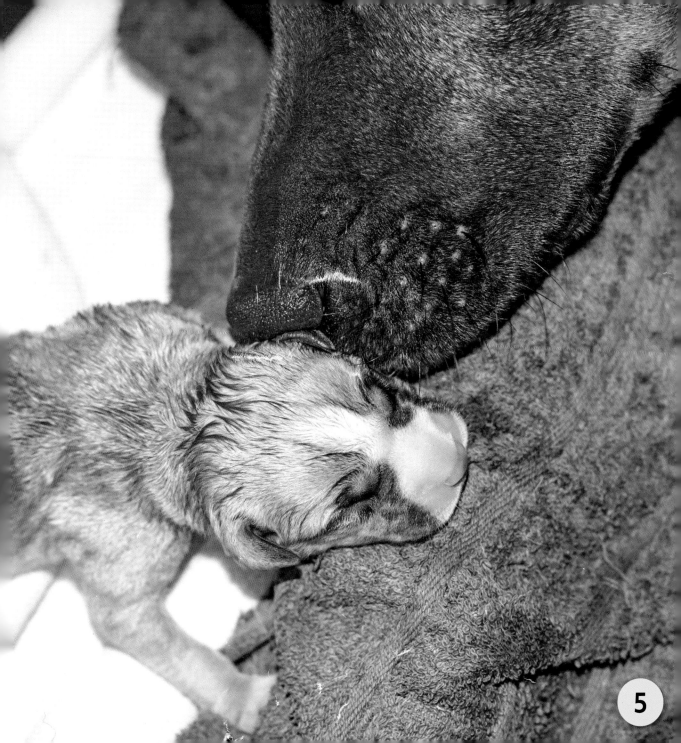

Soon, the mother has more puppies.

This group of baby dogs is called a **litter**.

The puppies are very small.

The babies can fit in a person's hand!

At first, the puppies cannot see or hear.

They sniff to find their mother.

They drink milk from her body.

Then, the puppies sleep in a big pile.

They sleep a lot.

When they wake up, they drink more milk.

This helps them grow!

After a few weeks, the puppies open their eyes.

They start to bark.

The puppies wag their tails.

In about a month, the puppies can eat **solid** food.

But they still need their mother's milk, too.

In another month, the puppies can leave their mother.

They learn to pee and poop outside.

Good job!

The puppies keep growing.

Some kinds of puppies grow into small dogs.

Some grow into really big dogs!

In about a year, the dogs are **adults**.

They can **mate**.

Then, there will be a new litter of puppies!

The Baby's Body

Ear

Eye

Nose

Tail

Paw

22

Glossary

adults grown-ups

breathe to take in air

litter a group of baby animals that are born together

mate to come together to have young

newborn a baby that was just born

solid something hard and firm

23

Index

Read More

Anthony, William. *My Dog (Me and My Pet).* New York: KidHaven Publishing (2020).

Schuetz, Kari. *Baby Dogs (Blastoff! Readers: Super Cute!).* Minneapolis: Bellwether (2014).

Learn More Online

1. Go to **www.factsurfer.com**
2. Enter "**Baby Dogs**" into the search box.
3. Click on the cover of this book to see a list of websites.

About the Author

Margaret Shanley rescued her dog Jerry when he was just nine weeks old. She takes Jerry everywhere she goes!